Dear Parent:
Your child's love of reading starts here!

Every child learns to read in a different way and at his or her own speed. Some go back and forth between reading levels and read favorite books again and again. Others read through each level in order. You can help your young reader improve and become more confident by encouraging his or her own interests and abilities. From books your child reads with you to the first books he or she reads alone, there are I Can Read Books for every stage of reading:

SHARED READING
Basic language, word repetition, and whimsical illustrations, ideal for sharing with your emergent reader

BEGINNING READING
Short sentences, familiar words, and simple concepts for children eager to read on their own

READING WITH HELP
Engaging stories, longer sentences, and language play for developing readers

READING ALONE
Complex plots, challenging vocabulary, and high-interest topics for the independent reader

ADVANCED READING
Short paragraphs, chapters, and exciting themes for the perfect bridge to chapter books

I Can Read Books have introduced children to the joy of reading since 1957. Featuring award-winning authors and illustrators and a fabulous cast of beloved characters, I Can Read Books set the standard for beginning readers.

A lifetime of discovery begins with the magical words **"I Can Read!"**

Visit www.icanread.com for information
on enriching your child's reading experience.

Runaway Ponies!

Library of Congress catalog card number: 2011934560
ISBN 978-0-06-208669-3 (trade bdg.)—ISBN 978-0-06-208667-9 (pbk.)
Typography by Sean Boggs

17 SCP 10 9 8 7 6 5 4 3   ❖   First Edition

I Can Read!™

READING
2
WITH HELP

Runaway Ponies!

PONY SCOUTS

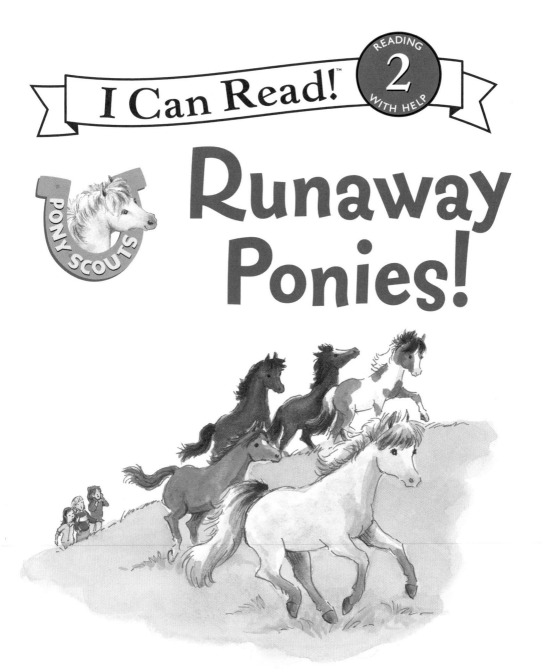

by Catherine Hapka
pictures by Anne Kennedy

HARPER

An Imprint of HarperCollinsPublishers

Meg's parents and baby brother
were going to visit relatives.
That meant Meg got to spend
the whole weekend
at her friend Jill's house.

She couldn't wait!

Jill lived on a pony farm,

and Meg loved ponies!

"Ready to go?" Meg's dad asked.

"I think so," Meg said.

"I packed my favorite toy horse
and my new horse book."

Meg's mom chuckled.

"That's good," she said.

"Did you pack your pajamas
and your toothbrush?"

Meg gasped.

"Oh, no, I forgot!" she cried.

She ran back upstairs to get them.

Jill was waiting for Meg
with their other friend Annie.
Meg, Annie, and Jill
called themselves the Pony Scouts.
"We're going to have so much fun!
Let's go see the ponies!" Meg said.

"Wait, Meg," Annie said with a giggle.

"Aren't you forgetting something?"

She pointed to Meg's suitcase

and sleeping bag.

The girls put Meg's things inside,

then went to the barn.

Jill's mom was already there.

"I need to bring the ponies in

for their breakfast," she said.

"Would you girls like to help?"

"Of course!" Meg said.

"I'll lead Sparkle."

Sparkle was Meg's favorite.

He was a spunky gray pony.

Jill's mom showed the girls
how to catch the ponies.
"Walk up to them
slowly and calmly," she said.
Meg led Sparkle, Jill led Apples,
and Annie led Splash.

"Be sure to latch
Sparkle's stall door, Meg,"
Jill's mom said.
"He likes to escape."

"Sparkle's already finished,"

Meg said a short while later.

"Can I groom him?"

"Of course," Jill's mom said.

"I'll be back soon, girls.

I forgot something in the house."

"I have an idea," Annie said.

"Let's visit Rosy and Surprise."

The cute bay pony and her foal

were still out in the field.

"Okay," Meg said eagerly.

She left Sparkle's stall,

then led the way outside.

For the next few minutes,

the girls watched Rosy and Surprise

frolic and play.

"Surprise is so cute!" Meg said.

Just then they all heard
a noise coming from the barn.
Jill turned to look.
"Oh, no!" she cried.
"Sparkle's loose!"

The girls rushed toward the barn.

"Did you remember to latch

his stall door when you came out?"

Jill asked Meg.

"Of course," Meg said.

Then she thought about it.

"At least, I think I did.

But maybe I forgot."

"Uh-oh," Jill said.

"Sparkle is very smart and playful.

Whenever he gets out,

he likes to open all the stalls."

Sure enough, the girls arrived

to see Sparkle opening Splash's door.

"Sparkle, no!" Meg cried.

But it was too late.

All the ponies trotted out

of the barn!

"Runaway ponies!" Annie cried.

"What should we do?" Meg cried.

"We've got to catch them!" Jill said.

They both started to run.

"Wait," Annie said.

"We need a plan.

I'll get Jill's mom

while you two catch the ponies.

Don't forget to bring lead ropes!"

"Good plan, Annie," Jill said.

Annie rushed toward the house.

Jill and Meg grabbed lead ropes,

then followed the ponies outside.

"Don't run or you might scare them,"
Jill warned.

"Just walk up to them slowly
and calmly like Mom taught us."

Meg and Jill followed the ponies.

Sparkle was still in the lead.

Meg wanted to run after him

before he went any farther.

But she made herself walk slowly
as Jill had reminded her.
Sparkle just stood there
and let her put a halter
and a lead rope on him.
What a relief!

Soon the ponies

were back in their stalls.

"I'm really sorry," Meg said.

"I forgot to latch Sparkle's door."

"It's okay, Meg," Jill's mom said.

"But I hope you'll remember

from now on."

"I promise I will," Meg said.

"Pony Scout's honor!"

After that, Meg still forgot things.

But she never forgot to latch

Sparkle's door ever again!

PONY POINTERS

grooming: using brushes and other tools to clean a pony or horse

lead rope: a rope used to guide a pony or horse

halter: something a pony or horse wears on its face to help people lead him or her